Angelina's Ballet Class

Story by Katharine Holabird

Illustrations by Catherine Kanner based on the illustrations by Helen Craig

PLEASANT COMPANY PUBLICATIONS™

Angelina is very excited. She's going to
Miss Lilly's ballet class today.

She packs her pink tutu and two pink
slippers in her ballet bag, and off she goes.

In the dressing room, Angelina meets
her friends. They love ballet class, too.
Angelina ties Alice's ribbons, and Alice
fixes Angelina's bow. In her tutu and
slippers, Angelina feels as light as a
feather. She can't wait to start dancing.

"Good morning, Miss Lilly!"
The ballerinas greet their teacher.

Angelina twirls around the dance studio
and then lines up with her friends.

Miss Quaver sits down and chooses some beautiful piano music to play for the lesson.

Just as the lesson is about to start, Cousin Henry appears, wearing his tiny slippers.

"You can follow Angelina," Miss Lilly says with a smile, and the piano music begins.

"Stretch and bend and touch your toes!" Miss Lilly shows her students how to warm up their muscles with exercises.

Angelina can touch her toes quite easily, but Henry still has trouble getting around his tummy!

Angelina stretches her legs
and turns out her feet.
Can you hold very still
like Angelina?

Alice stretches to the
ceiling, then touches
her toes. How high
can you reach?

Flora does the splits
and points her toes.
How far can you
stretch your legs?

Alice and Angelina link their hands and
touch their feet. Then they rock back
and forth to stretch their muscles.
Try this with a friend!

Felicity arches her back
and stretches her arms.
Can you bend back
as far as Felicity?

Miss Lilly claps her hands. "Now take your places at the barre, with backs straight and heads up."

Angelina and her friends hold the barre tightly and lift their legs higher and higher, until they can do beautiful arabesques just like Miss Lilly.

Henry tries to copy Angelina as she
checks her position in the mirror,
but he can't quite reach the barre!

All the dancers practice ballet positions together.

"First, second, third, fourth, fifth," repeats Miss Lilly. Angelina holds her arms above her head and balances in fifth position.

"Very good," Miss Lilly encourages everyone.

Henry gets confused, so Angelina helps him to cross his feet and stand very still.

First Position

Second Position

Third Position

Fourth Position

Fifth Position

"Now we'll take turns practicing leaps," Miss Lilly says with a smile.

Angelina is first in line. She loves to leap as high as she can—she feels as if she's flying across the room.

All the other dancers take their turns. Henry runs to keep up with them, then does his own funny jump.

"Bravo," Miss Lilly applauds.

"Point your toes and pirouette," Miss Lilly says.

The ballerinas follow her as she spins gracefully around the room.

Angelina starts to twirl very fast
and accidentally bumps into Alice.

Henry gets so dizzy, he has to sit down for a
minute. Sometimes pirouettes can be difficult!

Miss Lilly is very pleased with her ballet students. "Soon we'll give a recital for all the parents," she announces proudly.

Angelina and Alice are going to be the Sunflower Princesses. They try on their flower costumes and dance in front of the mirrors. Henry buzzes after them, pretending to be a busy bee.

elicity does a sideways leap called a *pas de chat* (pah de SHAH). *Pas de chat* means "cat step." Can you step like a cat, too?

Alice can do a lovely *arabesque* (ar-uh-BESK). She balances on tiptoe and lifts one leg straight behind her. If you stand on tiptoe, you can do an arabesque, too.

Angelina practices a *grand jeté* (gron juh-TAY). She loves to leap very high with her legs outstretched in the air. Can you leap as high as Angelina?

Flora does a graceful *pirouette* (peer-uh-WET). When she spins in a circle, she holds her head still. Can you pirouette like Flora?

Henry practices a *plié* (plee-AY). He bends his knees lower and lower and tries not to wobble. Try to bend way down like Henry, but don't wobble!

"All together now, listen to the music as we dance," Miss Lilly says.

She helps Angelina and her friends rehearse the movements for the "Sunflower Ballet" until they know every step by heart.

Henry can't remember his steps, so Angelina helps him by dancing like a bee, too.

When class is over, Angelina and the other ballerinas perform a *révérence* (ray-vay-RAHNS). This is a way to say thank you and good-bye to Miss Lilly.

Angelina does an elegant curtsy, and Henry does a formal bow. "Good-bye, Miss Lilly."

Miss Lilly waves to everyone. "See you next week!"

Angelina smiles. She can hardly wait to dance again with her friends at Miss Lilly's Ballet School.

See Angelina Dance!

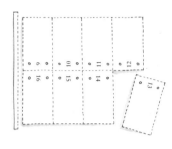

1. Remove the punch-out pages from the back of the book. Punch out each flip-book page.

2. Follow the page numbers to put the pages in order.

3. Tap the pages against a hard surface so that the right-hand edges align. This will make it easier to flip the pages.

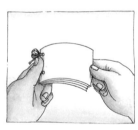

4. Keeping the right-hand edges aligned, bind the pages together with ribbons or brass fasteners.

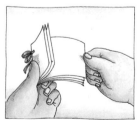

5. Bend the book down and let the pages flip up. You'll see Angelina dance!